THEIR GUARDED HEARTS

THE DIVIDED HEARTS SERIES
BOOK FOUR

MICHELLE BOLANGER

Published by Risen Fiction Publishing

7522 Timber Valley Dr

Franklin, OH 45005

www.RisenFiction.com

ISBN 978-1-969047-06-0 (Paperback)

eISBN 978-1-969047-07-7 (eBook)

Cover Art and Interior Design by Shonda Ramsey

Their Guarded Hearts by Michelle Bolanger was originally offered as a free newsletter incentive in 2017 with the title *The Dance* by Michelle Bolanger. Though the story line remains the same, it has been re-edited for clarity and readability.

Printed in the United States of America First Edition 2025

10 9 8 7 6 5 4 3 2 1

20251111

ONE

IVY

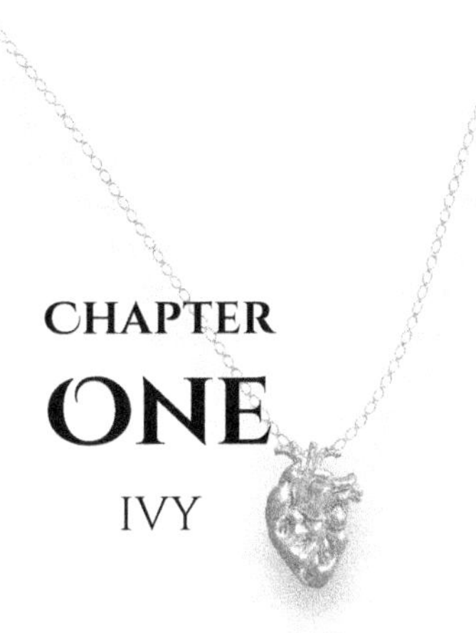

Ivy carried two cups of tea into the living room and watched her mom slide the last of the books she'd brought from storage into her new bookcase. For the last two years, they had been packed away because her ex-boyfriend, Wes, didn't like the dust they collected. Having all her autographed books back on display made the new apartment feel a little more like hers.

He wouldn't approve of the tiny space or the fluffy white dog padding behind her and begging for attention, but her choices were no longer his concern.

"I still don't understand why you need the dog." Her Mom scratched Tofu's head as she took the steaming mug. "You said Wes never hurt you."

"He didn't. Not physically, anyway." Ivy dropped onto the couch and propped a foot on her coffee table, stifling Wes' voice in her head telling her not to put her feet on the furniture.

"If he wasn't abusive, what happened?" her mom asked. "The two of you seemed happy."

"We might have been." She shrugged. "Until what I wanted wasn't what he wanted."

"All couples go through that," her mom said dismissively. "Your Dad can be impossible."

Ivy bit the inside of her cheek to keep from being angry. Her parents didn't understand why she'd broken up with such a successful guy, and Ivy supposed it was partly her fault. She'd kept the truth from them. In the beginning, she thought Wesley Matrone, a wealthy real estate mogul, simply wanted to take care of her. He spoiled her with a new wardrobe, offering to drive her to school in his luxury car, and by spending all his free time introducing her to his friends. After three years of it, she came to realize he had taken complete control over what she wore, where she went, and in the end, who she talked to.

She took a sip of her tea and wondered if her mom would believe her if she told her why she really had the dog.

"I caught Wes following me on the bike path." The snow-white Akita curled up at Ivy's feet. "Last week he almost talked the complex manager into giving him a key to my apartment," she said quietly.

"Wesley?" Her Mom jerked forward. "Are you sure it was him?"

"They have him on camera." She watched her mom's outright disbelief morph to doubt and then sighed. "I told you before, he's not the golden boy you think he is."

"No one thinks he is." Her Mom frowned. "But why would he track you down here?"

"I don't think he expected me to leave him." Ivy leaned her head back. "But telling him I was moving would have been a horrible idea."

"Are you sure? He took such good care of you." Mom reasoned. "He bought you so many nice things."

Ivy stifled her frustration, but her parents would think that was the measure of a good relationship. All her life they had struggled to give her the things she wanted. Meeting a man like Wes who could afford to give her the world was, to them, the best thing that could have happened to her. And it was, until the gifts turned her into another part of his immaculate image, and anything she had that didn't fit was unacceptable.

"He didn't just pay for the things. He picked them out. Everything. All the time." Ivy swallowed and absently ran her fingers through Tofu's fur. It was hard to describe how terrifying the last year with him had been, not to mention it was embarrassing that she hadn't realized it all so much sooner.

"He has great fashion sense and the money to buy nicer things than what we can afford. It only makes sense he would —"

"No, Mom." The statement sent her blood pressure up, and she blinked back frustrated tears. "It wasn't that I didn't like what he chose. It's the fact that I wasn't allowed to choose for myself." She met her mom's gaze, hoping she would understand. "He would get angry if I bought anything without him seeing it first."

"Maybe it was his way of helping you," she said though her expression was growing concerned.

"You aren't getting it." Ivy sat forward and reined in her anger. "He didn't buy me nice clothes or offer to drive me around to help me. He *told* me what to wear, drove me where *he* wanted me to go, and never let me out of his sight because he wanted to control everything about me. I wasn't his girlfriend; I was his possession."

Mom's cheeks darkened and her brow creased. "Why didn't you tell us?"

Ivy shook her head, was it her fault? "I don't know. I guess I was flattered someone like him would want me around at all. When he spent all that money and wanted to be with me all the time, I felt special."

"You are special." She touched Ivy's arm. "And apparently you were smart enough to know when to get out."

"Thank you." Ivy scratched the dog's belly. "I didn't feel very smart after I figured out what he was doing. I can't believe I let him control me for so long." She glanced around the apartment, took a deep breath and relaxed. "It's over, and I'm ready to move on." Tofu rolled to his back and pawed at her. "Besides, I have a new man in my life."

They both laughed when, as if in answer, the dog huffed a quiet bark then roo'ed until Ivy slid to the floor next to him.

"Well, it sounds like you did the right thing. I hate you being this far away, but your father and I are proud of you." Her Mom rose, and Ivy stood with her. "I need to get home, and you should get ready for your new job. Are you sure you can work both jobs?'

"It's only a couple days a week," she said. The new job at a specialty cosmetics shop would supplement her income until she picked up enough virtual assistant jobs to cover all her expenses. "The owner is really nice. He said he's looking forward to introducing me to his clients, and he even suggested one or two of them might be looking for an assistant."

"Just be sure to get out and have some fun." She kissed Ivy's cheek.

"I will." Ivy followed her mom to the door. Truth be told, she was looking forward to being alone.

CHAPTER

TWO

ZANE

Zane rolled onto his back and stretched. He fluffed the pillow under his neck and stared at the ceiling, in no hurry to get out of bed, let alone leave the house.

A soft weight hit the bed, and he wiggled his fingers under the sheet. Seconds later, his cat pounced, her claws and teeth furiously attacking his hand. He lay there until she grew tired of the game and padded onto his stomach. When she settled onto his chest, he peered up at her brilliant blue eyes.

Apple's soft meow made him smile. He'd found the tiny kitten hiding behind a stack of Granny Smith apple baskets at the edge of a farmer's market three years ago and promptly named her Burnt Apple Fritter because of her dark brown points and what he thought were bright green eyes that turned out to be blue. The vocal and demanding Siamese cat came into his life right after his disaster of a breakup with his last girlfriend. The kitten quickly took over his house and gave him someone to talk to when the empty rooms got too quiet.

He yawned; glad she was the only female he had to worry about. Instead of risking another broken relationship, he threw himself into his work choreographing for In The Arena and flirted when the mood struck him. He grinned as Apple purred loudly. Flirting was easy. It wasn't much different than dancing. As long as each participant followed the steps, it was harmless fun. Anything beyond that brought more drama than he was willing to deal with.

He was who he was, and he *liked* himself - no matter what label people tried to slap on him.

And there were plenty to choose from. Apple kneaded her paws into the comforter impatiently.

"Don't judge." He scratched her behind the ear before lifting her to the floor. "You get to sleep all day. Why shouldn't I?" She meowed once then trotted to the door and looked back expectantly. "Can I use the restroom first?" She meowed again. "Thank you for permission, your highness."

He kicked the covers aside and crossed to his bathroom. Apple followed a few steps behind, complaining loudly. He shooed her out of the sink twice while brushing his teeth. The second time, his makeup tray crashed onto the floor. His favorite foundation compact shattered and sent tiny bits of the makeup across the floor. He glared down at the cat grooming herself on the toilet seat.

"Was that really necessary?" She paused, tongue halfway down her leg. He imagined she shrugged, then continued preening as if she didn't care. "That was a brand-new compact." He scolded her as he cleaned up the mess. "Brandon's store is the only one that carries it, and you know he's always trying to set me up with one of his employees." He dusted off his hands and sighed. "I did place an order for the theater that needs picked up." Apple hopped back onto the counter and rubbed her head against his elbow. "I forgive you. I suppose now you want to eat?"

After feeding her and starting a kettle of water, he headed back to the closet that used to be his guest bedroom. The racks and shelves he'd installed were packed full but neatly arranged. Along the shorter back wall, he kept old costumes from some of his favorite stage shows and video shoots. Down the right side hung his jeans, button downs, dress pants, and a pair of custom-tailored suits. On the left were his everyday clothes, an eclectic collection of skirts, vests, t-shirts, and tight-fitting sweaters.

He flicked through the skirts, choosing an ankle length navy corduroy he hadn't had the chance to wear yet. He went back to the bathroom and laid out his makeup bag while Apple curled up in her customary spot in the sink to watch him. He scratched her thoughtfully.

Some of his friends claimed his failed relationships were intentional. They liked to suggest that if he would change his fashion choices, his life wouldn't be so complicated.

He smoothed black eyeliner above his lashes and sighed.

Wearing skirts and makeup wasn't a phase, a fashion statement, or a rebellious streak against society norms. Honestly, he didn't understand why more guys didn't wear skirts. In the summer months, kilts were more comfortable than shorts, and when it was cold, the ankle length options were like wearing a blanket.

He blended a swipe of darker brown eyeshadow over the gold in the crease his lid.

If the skirts weren't enough to tag him non-conforming, then his makeup routine certainly did. But, after all the years he'd spent on stage and in front of a camera, wearing makeup became a hobby.

The problem came when he put the two things together with the fact he was a heterosexual male, which also meant relationships got complicated quickly. His previous girlfriends were cool with his style - for a while. But when they realized he actually *liked* wearing skirts, and that he went through more makeup than they did, things usually ended with hateful names and slammed doors.

Apple never cared as long as her food bowl stayed full.

"You and me forever, right?"

She purred louder and blinked at him before rolling to her back. He tucked the foundation box in his front pocket and ran a hand over the cat's stomach. A split second later, her nails and teeth latched on.

"Coconut fudge, Apple! That hurts." He extricated his fingers and surveyed the damage. "Your affection is heartwarming."

The look she gave him was scathing as she slunk across the vanity and dropped to the floor.

"Remind me again why I keep you around?" His only answer was the swish of her tail as she disappeared down the hall. She was nowhere to be seen as he gathered his keys and wallet. "Have a nice day, honey," he called into the silent condo. "I'll call if I'm going to be late." On the front step, he paused realizing he had become one of 'those people,' and he couldn't stop the smile. It felt good to finally be happy with being single.

He parked in front of the shop and as soon as he got to the door, the store manager spotted him. Brandon's knowing grin and glance toward the back of the store told Zane the guy was indeed going to try setting him up with a new employee. Zane ran a hand down his mouth and stepped inside. Brandon conveniently disappeared down a side aisle with another customer, leaving him standing at the register. He exhaled, expecting Brandon to come back with the items he'd pre-ordered, but the wannabe Cupid was avoiding him.

In the angled mirrors of the store, he could see a brown-haired girl stocking lipsticks near the back. The only way out of this was to go meet her. If he was going in her direction, he might as well check out what was new on the shelves along the way. He pushed a pair of ear buds in and wandered toward her.

THREE

IVY

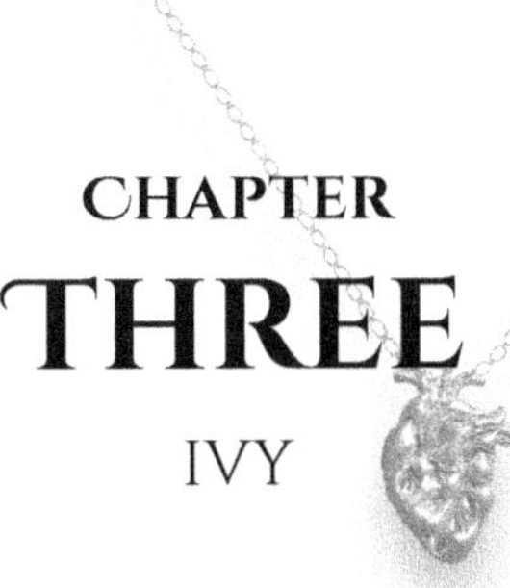

The bell over the door chimed, and Ivy glanced up. She was supposed to be watching the front counter, but the new shipment of lipsticks she was putting out for display distracted her. Stripes of color from the testers lined her forearm from the base of her palm nearly to her elbow. There were at least five colors she had to have. Thank goodness she got a decent discount. Getting the job here was more fun than she thought.

She glanced in the angled mirror to keep an eye on the customer and spotted a dark head one isle over near the eye shadows. Satisfied they were only browsing; she returned to slipping the narrow boxes into their labeled slots and hummed to herself. When she was finished, she tucked the empty box behind the counter and noted the customer a few feet away with their back to her. The snug t-shirt hugged what looked like a swimmer's body with wide shoulders that tapered toward a narrow waist and long legs hidden under an ankle length skirt. The customer half walked, half danced toward her in time to whatever music she was listening to. When she made a particularly suggestive hip swing, Ivy smiled and turned away before the girl caught her staring.

"Good morning," Ivy said brightly. "Can I help you find something?"

"Maybe. Are these new?" the customer asked without looking at her.

"The ones on the end are." Ivy pointed. "We just got them in last night."

"Did you try them all?" The girl's voice deepened.

"Almost." Ivy glanced at the smudged lines of color up her forearm and held a tester up to the corresponding line on her arm. "This one is my favorite. It's called Peach Tart." She snagged a disposable applicator. "Let's see what it looks like on you."

Collecting a small amount of the color on the spongy pad, Ivy looked up into a pair of deep brown eyes that were perfectly outlined in black liner and highlighted with a shimmer of yellow green that made the irises dance with flecks of gold. Her gaze caught on the dark triangle of a goatee, which set loose a swarm of butterflies in her stomach. Instead of recognizing what that meant and backing away like a smart girl, she impulsively smoothed the lipstick along the customer's full bottom lip.

A split second later, the rest of the man's handsome, very male face locked into focus.

He blinked but didn't retreat, and she braced herself for his reaction. She nearly lost feeling in her knees when his eyes darkened, and he pinched his lips together to spread the color as if savoring it.

"Peach Tart, you said?" His voice was low.

"I'm sorry," she stammered.

"For what?" He glanced in the mirror. "You were, right. I like the color."

"I didn't realize..." She trailed off, mortified.

"Realize what?" He looked down at his skirt, and the fluttering wings took flight in her stomach again when he gave her a lopsided smile. "Let me guess. You didn't realize I was a guy?"

"Well, no - I mean - I did when I saw your..." She touched the spot under her lip, then sighed and dropped the applicator into the waste basket on the counter. "I'm sorry. I hope I didn't offend you."

His laugh was rough, and the hair at the back of her neck prickled.

"Not likely." He offered his hand. "I'm Zane."

"I'm Ivy." She smiled weakly. "I truly didn't mean to offend - "

"The only way you can offend me is to keep insisting you offended me." He raised a perfectly defined brow. "Moving on?"

"Right." She snapped her mouth closed and gestured to the lipstick. "All the colors are created using natural pigments and are guaranteed not to smudge or smear for 24 hours." Her breath caught when he stepped closer and reached over her shoulder. She caught a whiff of woodsy cologne and shivered.

"Is this the one?" His breath was minty, and she noted with some satisfaction his hand wasn't completely steady as he held the box out.

"That's it." She nodded to the other items he carried and moved away before he could see the effect his closeness was having. "Is there anything else I can help you find?"

"No," he said with a chuckle that said he was enjoying her discomfort. "I think Brandon has the rest of my order."

She forced a smile and started toward the register. "Okay. I can check you out up front."

"You can't do that here?" he taunted.

Her breath caught, and she looked over her shoulder. His chin rose in challenge, and unable to resist, she pivoted toward him. He stood a few inches taller than her, making him about five-foot-nine to her five-foot-five. Black hair curled across his forehead, and she wondered if it was a soft as it looked. The goatee was his only facial hair, and when the line of his jaw feathered, her pulse sped up. His shoulders squared as if enjoying her attention, and she took in the rest of him. The pattern of his cream shirt accented his wide shoulders and narrow hips. It was untucked over a long, navy cotton skirt with five sharply stitched pleats down each leg. A fabric bag hung at one hip, the same color as the skirt.

"Aren't kilts usually shorter?" she challenged.

"This isn't a kilt, it's just sewn like one." His grin was mischievous. "I wear genuine kilts when I want to show off my legs."

Her cheeks heated as she wondered if they were as toned as his arms. "I might like to see that."

Zane blinked in surprise, then turned gracefully on his heel and stopped at the front register.

Oh gosh. She stared at his waiting back. *I said that out loud, didn't I?*

She stayed where she was, hoping Brandon would notice there was a customer waiting, but after a few thundering heartbeats, it was clear she was on her own. Zane seemed to be focused on his phone when she rounded the counter. The silence grew awkward as she scanned the foundation, concealer, and lip color.

"One Fifty-three seventy-four is your total," she said.

"Hey, Z," Brandon slipped behind the counter. "Here's the rest of your order."

Ivy scowled, then forced a smile when her boss handed her a box. She scanned the barcode. "The new total is $542.97."

"I gave you a 15% discount on the pre-order," Brandon said and nodded toward the back of the store. "Did you see we got some new lip color in today?"

"Thank you. I did see the new colors." Zane slid his card into the reader and flicked his gaze to hers. He pursed his lips and winked at her before smiling at Brandon. "Ivy here was very helpful."

Her cheeks warmed again, hotter this time, and she felt Brandon's attention on her. The card machine beeped, and Ivy handed him his receipt, proud her hand wasn't shaking. As he took it, his finger brushed along her palm in a way that had to be intentional, sending sparks up her forearm. She curled her hand back and glanced nervously at Brandon whose eyes narrowed. She wanted to crawl into the back room and never come out. She bagged

Zane's purchase, and the two men moved to the end of the counter.

Brandon smirked at her, then refocused on Zane. "I heard you're choreographing a new show for Arena."

"I am." Zane pointed to the white earphone cord at his neck. "This last track is going to be amazing if Dani and I can ever get the timing right."

Ivy froze as his identity sank in. *Zane Parish.* He was the lead dancer and co-choreographer for *In the Arena*, a nationally acclaimed professional dance troop. Last month, they were named one of the hottest hip-hop groups in the nation. On his own, Zane was tied to some of the biggest names in music, and she could count at least three major music videos featuring him as a dancer.

While he and Brandon chatted about the new project, she tried not to be obvious as she watched him. Her mouth went dry when he braced an arm against the counter, making the deeply defined muscles of his arm flex. It was obvious why the camera loved those arms - and the rest of him. In his last music video appearance, his neatly stacked abs and contoured back had gotten most of the screen time as a female singer crooned a sad ballad. Try as she might, she couldn't remember the singer's name, not with his bare triceps flexing inches from her.

"Thank you for all your help today, Ivy." Zane's gaze swept over her, and he gave her a sly smile before he walked out the door.

She watched him go and tried to ignore Brandon's curious stare.

"What was that?" he asked.

"What was what?" She kept her face carefully neutral as she faced him.

He pinned her with an exasperated look. "Did you not notice he was flirting with you?"

"No, he wasn't," She brushed past him. "You're imagining things."

"I don't think so," Brandon sing songed. "I saw the whole thing." Blood pounded through her ears when he hooked a thumb toward the angled mirrors surrounding the store. "You two couldn't keep your eyes off each other."

She hesitated, then kept walking. "You're making it up. I was helping a customer, and he was just being nice."

"Ten bucks says he comes back looking for you," Brandon called. "I give him three days."

"I'll take that bet," she replied.

He might flirt, but someone like him wouldn't be interested in a girl who worked at a makeup counter. She bit her lip and looked at the one empty slot under Peach Tart then toward the door. She touched her stomach, willing the butterflies to settle and hoping her boss was right.

FOUR

ZANE

Zane stared at the two remaining Euchre cards in his hand, trying to remember which suit his sister, Dani, called as trump.

As reigning champs three years in a row, he and Dani were not allowed to talk at all unless it was their turn to call. The rest of the basement party room was full of their brothers and their wives for the annual Parish Euchre tournament. Baden, Dani's intended, was seated beside him, paired with their youngest brother, Zachary. Both of them were smiling faintly, likely knowing Zane hadn't heard a word that was said all night. This was the final hand, and he and Dani were about to be eliminated.

He looked up, but her death stare told him there would be hell to pay if he chose the wrong card again. He ran a thumb nail across his forehead and pulled out the five of clubs.

The moment his card was on the pile, Dani tilted her head. "Really? That's the card you're going to kill me with?"

"Shut it!" Baden and Zach said in unison.

Two more cards hit the table, then Baden raked the cards to him.

Unless Dani held something higher than his three of hearts, they had lost.

"Hand them over!" Baden said and they all dropped their remaining cards on the table.

"You. Outside." Dani stood and pointed to the patio door as Baden and Zach high-fived. "I'll deal with you later." She flicked Baden's ear and dodged his halfhearted swat.

Zane did as she commanded. The outside air was refreshing, and for a moment he enjoyed the feel of the cool breeze. Until Dani punched him in the arm.

"You either threw off every hand or wasted trump on a stupid trick." She crossed her arms. "Who is she?"

"No one." Zane rubbed his bicep but avoided her eyes.

"Look me in the face and say that."

"No."

"Then answer my question. I wanna know who the chick is that cost us the trophy." Her pout made him huff a laugh, and she hit him again.

"Stop it." He stepped out of range. "I flirted with a new girl at the cosmetics store yesterday. It's nothing."

"Do you know her name?" She challenged. "And remember, you can't lie to me."

He wrinkled his nose. Having a sister who could read his intentions with a sniff was majorly annoying sometimes.

"You do!" Her eyes widened. "Come on, Z."

"Her name is Ivy." Dani nodded for him to continue, and he bristled. "So what? I don't have to forget every cute girl's name just to prove I'm not interested."

"Hair color?"

"Light brown."

"Eyes?"

"Hazel."

Dani's brow rose. She had made her point. He was smitten, and she wasn't going to let up until he told her the whole story.

His skin tightened remembering the way Ivy had impulsively applied the lipstick. "What was I supposed to do? Be mean?" He raked his hair back. "She looked absolutely mortified after she did that." He grinned. "It was the most adorable thing ever."

"Are you going to ask her out?"

"You know I'm nothing but a flirt." He cringed internally. That was an accusation leveled at him more than once when he refused to let a date up his skirt. He snorted at his own joke, but Dani was having none of his deflection.

"You called her cute and adorable." She ticked them off on her fingers. "You remembered not only her name but also her —"

"All right!" He waved her off. "I might be...interested in her."

Dani paused and an odd look crossed her face. "We need to make sure she's not a fugitive or something. Find out what information you can get from Brandon before you get too involved."

"A fugitive? Where did that come from?" He watched her in amusement.

"I don't know. I think that's the only kind of crazy you haven't dated."

"Thanks, Sis."

"Not your fault. Women are nuts." She waved a hand. "Maybe I should go meet — "

"Absolutely not. You are the kind of crazy that will send her running."

She shot him a mocking smile. "I can be charming when I want to be."

He let his gaze drift over the back yard. "I'm not asking Brandon. If I see her again, I'll see what happens. I'm in the store often enough, but I'm not going to force it."

"Are you sure you don't want me to check her out?" she offered.

Between his sister's hacking skills and Baden's cyber security connections, they would be able to find out nearly everything about her in minutes. For a brief second, the thought crossed his mind, but he quickly dismissed it.

"Don't do that." He threw an arm over her shoulders. "I'll keep you posted."

She leaned contentedly into him for a moment, then whacked him in the stomach. He grunted and stepped away. "What was that for?"

"Baden and Zach are going to win this tournament, and I have to live with both of them. Do you have any idea how much payback I'm due?" She stalked into the house, letting the screen door crack shut behind her.

Zane chuckled then sat on the stairs and stretched his legs out in front of him. Other than Ivy's initial embarrassment at misidentifying him as a girl, his clothing and makeup hadn't seemed to bother her. In fact, she'd even teased him in a positive way about his skirt. He leaned back on his elbows to stare at the sky. The stars were bright out away from the city lights. It had been over a year since he'd last dated, and longer than that since he'd brought a girl to the homestead. Having fifteen brothers and dozens of cousins constantly in and out of the house was hard to explain away as normal, and being a non-conforming heterosexual male didn't help.

As the ruckus continued in the house behind him, he wondered if he would ever meet someone who would accept him and his family.

FIVE

IVY

I vy wrinkled her nose at the faint chemical smell as she entered the thrift store and waved to the manager. It was Tuesday, the day most of the new items arrived. Some weeks she went home with arm loads, and other times she spent an hour in the dressing room only to leave with nothing. Either way, it was an easy way to kill an evening.

She pushed a wiggly blue cart between the rows of t-shirts and workout clothes. There was a steady stream of other shoppers who also knew today was new merch day, and she wove between them, tossing a few tank tops and a pair of running shorts into the basket. A large rounder of skirts was at the end of the row, and she paused to flick through them. She walked a few steps from her cart, pulling out a couple she wanted to try and absently dropped them into the closest basket then froze when a familiar deep voice spoke.

"I like the style, but I don't think those will fit me." Zane Parish leaned causally against the rounder, and the amusement on his face sent a zing of electricity through her.

She shrugged. "How would you know unless you try them on?"

"Well, you are pretty good with color." He held up one of her choices. "Peach seems to be a favorite of yours."

Her cheeks burned, but she met his gaze. "I did tell you it would look good on you."

"And you were right." His eyes darkened mischievously. "Were you shopping for me or for you?"

She glanced at his cart then hers. "Both apparently."

"I've never had a personal shopper before. Maybe I've been missing out." She swallowed when he stepped closer. His expression went from playful to genuine. "I was on my way to the dressing room. I'd appreciate your opinion."

His eyes were a lustrous brown, and she wanted to ask if he'd chosen the soft gold along his upper lid for the sole purpose of making the flecks of green around his iris stand out, but she couldn't make words form when his lip quirked up in a sexy smirk.

"Ivy?" he prompted.

She managed a nod and squeaked, "Sure." His laugh made her toes curl, and she cleared her throat as he turned away.

He parked both the carts next to an empty bench outside the dressing rooms then gestured to his. "Make your first selection."

"What?" She raised a brow, which he mirrored.

"Pick something and I'll try it on."

She bit her lip and tentatively sorted through his pile. She held out an orange polo shirt and a pair of navy shorts. When he cocked his head in challenge, she ticked her chin toward the empty room behind him.

"You picked those yourself," she said.

He exhaled through his nose and closed himself in the room. When the door latched, she raccooned through his cart to see what else he'd chosen. As she noted sizes and colors, she pieced together a couple more outfits. He opened the dressing room door with a flourish, and she giggled when he struck a pose.

"The navy fabric of the shorts is all natural, and the color is guaranteed not to fade for at least a hundred years. If I keep it that long it might even come back in fashion." He mock frowned. "You're gonna have to do better than this if you want to call yourself a personal shopper."

"I didn't call myself that," she said indignantly and held out a short gray skirt and matching red and gray plaid button up. "You did."

He surveyed the pieces then shook his head. "Closer, but no." He stepped near enough that she felt the heat of his skin. She didn't move when he braced a hand on her shoulder and reached around her to pick up a pair of black skinny jeans.

He pointed into her cart. "Hand me that yellow tank top, please?"

She did as he asked, adding weakly, "It's too small."

He draped it over his shoulder with a grin that sent tingles all along her spine. "Trust me," he said as he plucked the skirt from her hand.

The door clicked shut behind him, and she tried not to listen to the rustle of fabric as he changed clothes a few feet away. She chewed her lip and studied the pile of clothes wanting to pinch herself. She was thrift store shopping with Zane Parish.

Trying not to look obvious, she sniffed the fabric at her shoulder where his woodsy sent still clung. Her eyes slid partway closed, then snapped open when hip hop music suddenly blared from behind her. She whirled around as Zane danced out of the dressing room. His eyes were locked on hers and the taunting look in them combined with his smooth movements made her jaw drop open.

Over top of the black skinny jeans, the gray skirt hit him about mid-thigh, and she was right about the tank. It was too small, but she couldn't look away. She tried to remember how to breathe as her eyes followed the line of his collar bones down to the well-defined edges of his pecs where the skin disappeared below the low-cut collar. The thin fabric did nothing to hide the way his chest muscles rippled as he moved, and his lean arms were sharply cut and laced with veins that made her fingers itch to trace the patterns criss crossing his forearms.

"This is more like it." He turned off the music and jerked to a stop as he tipped his head toward her. He broke the pose and frowned. "Is something wrong? You look like I kicked you."

She opened and closed her mouth, but no sound came out.

"Ivy?" His Adam's apple bobbed.

She tore her gaze away from his exposed skin and complemented on the first thing she could think of.

"You look great in those jeans," she managed.

He stiffened, then his shoulders dropped.

"Thanks. I get that a lot." The ice in his tone cut like knives before he shook his head and vanished into the dressing room.

"What did you just say?" she whispered.

The dressing room door opened, and his expression revealed nothing. He held out the yellow tank. "You were right. It's too big."

"Too small." She said reflexively but didn't take it from him. She met his flat stare evenly. "That was the best part of the whole outfit." He rolled his eyes, and she crossed her arms. "Did I say something wrong?"

He met her gaze again, then pointedly tossed the jeans on the discard pile. "It doesn't matter."

"It does to me," she said firmly.

He snorted. "I have to go."

"Hold on," she snapped. His glare almost made her take a step back, but she lifted her chin. "You promised to pick outfits for me when you were done."

"No, I didn't."

She tossed her hair. "Not directly, but it was implied. I apparently chose poorly. Now it's your turn."

He did that sexy jaw tick thing guys did, nearly making her knees buckle, then his eyes slid over her as if he was considering her challenge.

"Fine," he gritted and swung his gaze over the store before he brushed past her. "I'll be right back."

"I - I'll wait here. I have some other things to try." Her voice died out as he disappeared toward the front of the store.

She blindly picked a shirt and shorts from her cart and stepped inside the dressing room. Dropping onto the bench, she threw the clothes in the corner. She'd known him all of three seconds and could easily see someone, or multiple someones, had hurt him, but she still wasn't sure what she had done to make him turn so cold.

There was nothing she could do now, and sulking in a dressing room felt very kindergarten-ish. She picked up the items she had thrown and opened the door. Unsurprisingly, Zane was nowhere in sight. She hung their discarded choices on the return rack and left the empty carts at the front.

SIX

ZANE

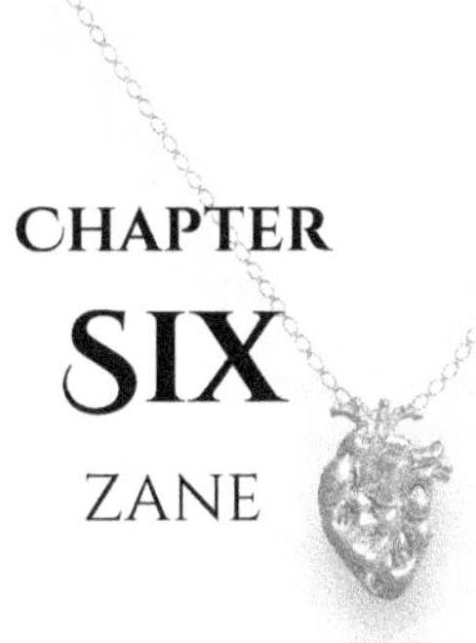

Zane stalked across the street and into a tiny restaurant. He slid into an empty table near the front window and glared at the thrift store's front door. Ivy exited a few minutes later, and he watched until she disappeared around a corner then rocked back in his chair and blew out a breath.

She was beautiful and funny, but what intrigued him most was the way she instinctively followed his lead in the flirting dance he enjoyed so much. She even surprised him by adding a few flourishes of her own that kept him on his toes.

Her compliment on the jeans was innocent, but he'd instinctively thrown up his defenses. The implication behind her words had been the death knell of every other relationship, and he wasn't about to go through it again. He glanced in the direction she'd gone and bit his lip. If he were willing to be honest with himself, he knew that wasn't her intent. Especially when, despite his little temper tantrum, she'd tried to resume the flirting dance. The corner of his mouth twitched at the way she'd stood like a toddler with her hands on her hips and demanded he honor a deal they hadn't made.

A noisy group of college students entered the restaurant, filling the small space with laughter. Since he had no intention of ordering anything, he left. He could stew at the theater where it was quiet.

Based on the music playing in the main amphitheater when he entered through the backstage door, Dani was working with one of the new groups. Though he wanted to check it out, she would corral him into helping with the choreography. For the first time in a while, he wasn't in the mood to dance. Instead, he changed into a pair of basketball shorts headed for the weight room. It took forty minutes of increasing speed and incline on the treadmill before he got Ivy out of his mind. But the moment he heard one of the girls out front laugh, she was back at the center in his thoughts.

He grabbed a jump rope and set a blistering pace. Sweat ran down his back as he dropped the jump rope and snagged a towel from the bin. The music stopped and the back door slammed shut over and over as the participants left.

He was vaguely aware of his sister's assessing presence at the door, but he ignored her. Instead, he loaded a barbel and positioned himself on the bench. He finished two sets before she spoke.

"You only work this hard when a girl ticks you off." Dani strode across the room. "What did she do?"

He slammed the weight back in place. "She told me I looked good in jeans."

"Of course you look good in jeans." Dani smoothed a hand down her thigh. "I mean, not as good as I do, but still."

"Wait." He sat up on the bench, pointing to her legs. "Are those my jeans?"

She twisted to look at the back pockets, then gave him an innocent look. "They used to be your favorite pair, I think."

"Remind me to get my house key back," he muttered.

"But your closet is much more interesting than mine. Besides, Apple would let me in. I bring her treats." She sat in front of him on the bench. "Do you like her?"

"Apple? Depends on the day." He pushed her off then lay back down.

She kicked his shin. "I don't know why I put up with you. This Ivy girl, do you like her?"

He concentrated on the movements of his exercise to avoid answering, then grunted when she kicked him again. His lip curled in a grin when she swore under her breath.

He finished his reps and sat up. "I do, and that's the problem," he sighed.

She flung her arms out. "How exactly is that a problem?"

"Come on, Sis. I'm not exactly normal." She glared at him, but he stopped her. "I'm being serious. Girls think it's cute that I like to talk about makeup or shop for skirts with them. For a while. Then they always try to change me." He stood and re-racked the weights. "After the last fiasco, I'm not ready to try again."

"I told you that girl was trouble. Even Baden knew she wasn't wired straight, and he only met her once. Ask this Ivy girl out." She folded her arms. "When was the last time you had one of Devon's steaks? Take her there. If she doesn't like his restaurant, you can bail."

"And I'll be out a hundred and fifty with nothing to show for it." He moved her aside and picked up a yoga mat. "That's not a fair test. Taking a girl to a five-star restaurant for the first date is a bit excessive, don't you think?"

"If she's the right one, then the dollar menu will be perfect. Just ask her out." She kissed his cheek, then grimaced. "Ugh. You're sweaty."

"Duh."

"I want a full report." She headed for the exit. "And I apologize ahead of time if Apple is acting funny when you get home."

"You'll be the first call I make when she...wait. What did you give my cat this time?"

"Catnip might have been on sale." She dodged the roll of tape he tossed at her and hit the door with her backside. "Wear the sandalwood cologne I left on the counter. Girls *love* a great smelling man."

The door almost closed behind her, but it reopened, and she leaned inside. "Hey, Z?"

"What?" He flicked the mat out and smoothed it with a toe.

"Never change, okay?" Her tone made him look up. "You're the best brother ever, and any girl would be lucky to have you." Mushy compliments weren't her style, and her words made his throat burn.

"Thank you."

CHAPTER
SEVEN

IVY

Ivy headed for the accessory section and hoped the nearly deserted thrift store would serve as a distraction from her obsession with Zane. But as she browsed the store, she found herself looking for things he might like. By the time she got to the back of the store, she'd tossed a long, blue, pinstripe skirt, a white button up shirt, and a gray vest in her cart and told herself they were for her.

She put the outfit in a dressing room to try on, then absently flipped through a rack of scarves beside the shoes. She tossed a couple onto a wingback chair someone had conveniently dragged in front of the mirrors.

Last night, she'd watched hours and hours of Zane and In The Arena's YouTube videos, eventually falling asleep to dream about what it would be like to dance with him. Watching the away he danced amazed her. He flowed seamlessly from choppy hip hop to fluid modern dance, to sensual music videos seemingly without effort. Her cheeks burned remembering how she'd dreamed of being in one of the racier videos with him. She wanted to be the girl who got to feel his bare skin as they moved in perfect rhythm to the music.

"Ridiculous," she muttered and slipped one of the scarves over her head. "Why would Zane Parish want to dance with me?"

"Because everyone should dance once in a while."

Ivy's breath caught as she met Zane's gaze in the mirror's reflection. He leaned casually on the back of the wing chair, and his lopsided smile sent wild flutters through her stomach.

"What if I step on your toes?" she challenged.

His low chuckle made her skin prickle. "It wouldn't be the first time or the last." He tilted his chin thoughtfully. "Wouldn't the white one match your shirt better?"

She bit her lip to hide her excited grin and adjusted the eggplant purple scarf. "True, but I prefer something a little less...common." She held her breath, hoping he would understand.

His expression warmed, then mischief flared in his eyes. "Well, that expands my outfit options."

He stepped around the chair, running his long fingers across the curved back of it. She tracked the motion of his hand as a sudden desire to be a chair struck her. The fluttering in her stomach increased when he paused beside her.

"I'm sorry I ran out the other day," he said softly.

"Why did you?" she blurted.

He made a humming sound. "Because different is good until this kind of different isn't what people want anymore." He straightened the belt at the top of his dark green kilt, and he might have said something else, but all she could focus on were how great his legs looked. "Ivy? My eyes are up here."

She jerked her attention to his face as her cheeks heated. His smirk was infuriatingly adorable.

"I'm sorry." She waved a hand along the length of him. "You have great looking legs."

He crossed his arms and raised a sculpted eyebrow. "And the rest of me?"

His perfectly contoured makeup accentuated the masculine line of his jaw, and his signature eyeliner and shadow combination made his eyes sparkle. Every part of him was undeniably gorgeous, and her mouth went dry when he alternately flexed his forearms, but the intentionality of the movements was too obvious to let pass.

She lifted a shoulder. "I can probably get used to it."

"What makes you think I'll let you?"

"You keep coming back," she replied and hoped the relaxed flirting lasted this time.

"Guess I'm a sucker for a pretty face." He touched her cheek and for a second she thought he might kiss her. Instead, he moved her to the side and checked himself out in the mirror. "I mean, who wouldn't want to look at this all the time?"

"I like you in a skirt. I mean...the skirts don't bother me," she stammered. He froze for a second and didn't look at her. When he didn't answer she continued. "I'm sorry if my comment the other day offended you."

His gaze slid to hers, and her heart stumbled at the brief flash of vulnerability in his expression. "You didn't offend me."

"Someone did."

"Moving on." He snagged her cart and rested a hand on her shoulder. "Let's see if we can find you a proper outfit."

Her heart stopped, and she nearly bolted for the door. He couldn't know that was the exact phrase Wes used when he deemed an outfit she chose unpresentable. Robotically, she allowed Zane to guide her a few racks over and watched as he considered then moved past several choices before laying something in the cart. Her chest constricted, but she fought back the panic. Zane wasn't Wes, and his own clothing choices made it clear he wasn't overly concerned with what people thought, but the implication of his words wouldn't go away.

Wes's voice echoed, filled with distain. *"I have an image, Ivy, and in public I expect you to uphold it."* How many times had she heard some variation of that?

She followed Zane a few racks over and tried to remember what her counselor had told her about speaking up for herself. He sorted through a line of shirts, considering a couple before pulling one out and tossing it in the cart.

"Please don't say it like that." She hated the squeak in her voice and cleared her throat as she stepped toward him. "There is nothing wrong with what I'm wearing."

"That's true." His questioning eyes slid over her face and narrowed slightly. "Did I say anything was wrong with what you have on?"

"No." She lifted her chin. "I just don't like being told what I can and can't wear."

He raised an eyebrow and glanced down at himself. "I'm not sure why you think I would do that."

You wouldn't. She exhaled and scratched her forehead, then jumped when he touched her arm.

He tipped his head to meet her gaze. "You asked me to pick something for you before I ran out like a jerk." His mouth twitched up, and she flushed at the color on his full lips. *Peach Tart.* The mischief was back in his eyes as he dropped his hand and moved closer. His nearness sent her pulse racing. "I thought we were just having fun."

"We were. We are. I'm sorry." She swallowed and dropped her gaze.

"You keep saying that." He eased back, and she breathed easier. "Why do you apologize for standing up for yourself?"

Her throat tightened. "It's not something I'm good at."

He snorted. "Sure you are." He didn't look at her, but she sensed he saw her more clearly than anyone ever had. "My guess is that you've just been made to feel bad for doing it." He dropped some clothes into the cart and lowered his voice. "Believe me when I tell you no one should have that much power over you."

When their eyes met, his were completely unguarded. It was clear, even without knowing anything about her and Wes, he understood. Then the moment was gone, and he was sorting through the rack again.

Ivy joined him in flipping hangers aside absently. Despite the knowledge he was only doing what she'd asked him to do, letting him pick an outfit for her still felt like she was handing herself back to Wes. "You don't have to do this. I was only trying to get you to stay."

"I know, but I said I would, and a deal is a deal." He held out his selections; a pair of red and black plaid leggings, an oversized black tank top, and a pair of black, wedge sole boots covered with straps and narrow silver buckles. All of it was so completely unlike anything Wes would ever let her wear; she relaxed and took the items from him.

She took in the way his posture had changed. It was subtle, but he had clearly retreated from their earlier banter. It wasn't hard to imagine why. How often had people criticized him for wearing skirts or mocked him for wearing makeup? And she had just tried to accuse him of doing the same to her. A tiny bit of indignation wound through her.

"Zane, I'm -"

"Don't." He cut her off then ran his tongue over his lower lip and looked away. "You don't have to apologize."

"They should have," she said quietly.

"Moving on," he said firmly.

"Not until you accept my apology," she retorted.

"I just said you have nothing to apologize for."

"But -"

"Are you going to argue with me, or try these on?" His face softened, and he pointed behind her. "Add the leather jacket."

She exhaled and took the clothes from him. "Fine."

"And no cheating." He smirked and crossed his arms. "Love it or hate it, you have to show me."

EIGHT

The ferocity of her expression made Zane's heartbeat so hard he was sure she could hear it. As if her stunning multicolored eyes and the easy way her skin flushed when he got close wasn't enough to arrest his curiosity, she was the kind of paradox he discovered he couldn't resist. When it came to her own thoughts and opinions, she blushed and stumbled over her words, but in the next breath she sounded ready to take on the world to defend his. He'd never met anyone like her.

And was it possible she truly did understand what it was like to have every choice you made questioned? She glanced at the clothes, and he hated the way her shoulders dropped.

"One outfit." He nodded to the dressing room. "Then our deal is done, and you never have to see me again." His stomach tightened when she looked relieved and then a little disappointed. "Unless you want me to keep coming back."

"Of course I do," she said quickly, then blushed. Her gaze narrowed when he smirked, likely realizing what he'd just gotten her to admit. "I'm going to try these on and then you are free to go."

"A deal is a deal," he replied and dropped into the chair.

The door closed and latched behind her, and heat flooded his body when he realized she was undressing only a few feet away. This girl was under his skin, and he couldn't explain why, but something about her ignited a protective streak in him he didn't know he had. There was a vulnerability to her underneath her bold words, and he wanted to know more. He deliberately stood and walked to a nearby shoe rack.

Dani accused him of being smitten with her, but this was more than that. She fascinated him.

"Zane?" Ivy's tone sounded genuinely worried, and he realized he'd wandered further from the dressing room than he'd intended. He rounded the shoes and stood quietly behind the chair.

Under the door, he could see her buckling on the boots as she muttering something. He wondered if she knew she talked to herself.

"Zane?" she called again. "Are you still there?"

He bit back a laugh when she stomped a foot at his silence.

The door cracked open, and she peered out. Her gaze found his, and she started to retreat.

He shook his head and curled a finger. "No cheating."

Her lips thinned, and he almost laughed again at the spark of annoyance in her eyes. But when she drew a breath and stepped into full view, his stomach tightened.

The wedge boots lengthened her legs, and the plaid leggings hugged them like a second skin. The black tank top he'd chosen fell past her hips, but it was nearly sheer, and without the leather jacket, the outline of her curves stopped his breath for a moment.

"I forgot the jacket." Ivy's voice wavered, and he snapped his gaping mouth closed. Her cheeks pinked, but she held his gaze, challenging him to look anywhere else.

He didn't, but only with effort. "You don't need it." His voice was rougher than he'd intended, and her blush deepened in response.

She crossed her arms as if to cover herself, and she shifted uncomfortably from foot to foot. "It fits, but I don't know where I would ever wear something like this."

"How about to dinner?" he asked. "With me."

Surprise brightened her face, then her eyes narrowed. He braced himself for her rejection.

"Do I get to pick your outfit?"

For a split second, his defenses flared, but he pushed them aside and lifted a shoulder. "Fair is fair, I suppose."

Her gaze darted to the side, then back as a taunting smile curved her lips. She stepped into the dressing room. The door clicked, and cloth rustled as she changed.

"When?" she asked from inside.

"When what?" he replied.

She emerged carrying the clothing he'd picked for her.

"When are you taking me to dinner?" she asked.

He tucked his hands into his front pockets. "Are you busy tomorrow?"

"I am now." She turned to walk backwards but stopped him when he tried to follow. "Your outfit is in the dressing room." She headed for the register. "503 Jackson Place. It's right around the corner. Pick me up at 6."

Dread threatened to creep up his neck as he opened the dressing room door, but when he spotted what she'd left behind, he hurried inside to try it all on.

NINE

Ivy's townhouse was in a row of narrow brownstone style buildings on a quiet side street a few blocks from the thrift store. Zane's nerves jangled as he knocked on the door and was greeted by a flurry of excited barking and the scrape of nails on what sounded like tile. He didn't hear anything other than the dog and was about to ring the doorbell but jumped back when a white muzzle poked through the mail slot at about knee level.

"Tofu!" Ivy's voice carried though the open slot. "Get back." There was more scrabbling of nails on the floor as the dog's nose vanished.

He braced himself when she unlocked and opened the door, prepared to see a dog straining at the end of her arm. Instead, a huge white dog with a head like a bear sat calmly behind her, its fluffy white tail lashing back and forth across the travertine floor of a small entry way.

Ivy swept the hair off her forehead and turned apologetically. "Sorry about that. I didn't get to him fast..." Her voice trailed off and her eyes widened in appreciation. "It actually fit?"

"Close enough." He smoothed a hand down the front of the gray vest and straightened a pleat in the skirt. "My tailor adjusted the waist a bit last night, but nothing major."

"Your tailor?" Something odd flashed across her face.

"She does the costuming at the theater," he said. "Bad experience with a tailor?"

"No." She tucked a strand of hair back. "It's a long story."

The dog scooted forward on its haunches, stretching his twitching nose toward him. He extended the back of his hand. "Husky?"

"Akita." Ivy rested a hand on the dog's head as he sniffed him. "Another long story."

He scratched the dog's chin. "I'd love to hear it."

"Not tonight." She shooed the dog away from the door and slipped her purse over a shoulder. "Ready?"

He stepped aside, then offered his arm. "Do you like steak?"

"I do." She placed her hand into the bend of his elbow as they stepped outside.

"Then you are going to love Devon's place. I've known him for years." He waited as she closed and locked the door, noting the extra deadbolt. "I thought this was a pretty safe neighborhood."

When she tensed for the third time, a flag of concern waved at the back his mind.

"It is safe. I guess I'm just a little paranoid." Her smile was tight when she looked up at him. "Where did you park?"

He searched her eyes for a moment. Sensing there was more to the story than simple paranoia, his concern increased, and he couldn't help wondering if he should have let Dani look into her. It was too late now. They descended the few steps, and he ticked his head toward the shopping center.

"Actually, it's a nice night, and the restaurant is only a few blocks away behind your store. Do you mind walking?"

"Not at all." She didn't hesitate and he relaxed a bit as they fell in step.

The shopping center that housed the makeup store backed up to a series of older buildings that had been renovated into high end shops, apartments, and restaurants. Devon's steakhouse had been one of the first to go into the upscale area, and seating filled up quickly even on weeknights, and was strictly by reservation only. Zane pulled a few strings to get a semi-private table, hopefully to avoid him being recognized though the staff usually did a great job running interference for any celebrities dining with them.

Zane held open the door. "We're a little early, but they don't look too busy." He waited for Ivy to step inside and turned when she hesitated, paling slightly. "Is something wrong?"

She stared at the inscription on the glass entry wall. He followed her line of sight and scanned the list etched into the glass. Alongside the names of the businesses housed inside were the building owner's names and a short dedication memorial to the city founder. She lifted her gaze to look up the side of the six-story brick building and swallowed before dropping her gaze to his. The thin layer of fear in her eyes made him step closer to her as his concern morphed into protectiveness.

He ticked his head back the way they'd come. "We can go somewhere else if you want."

"No." She squared her shoulders. "This is perfect," she said though a forced smile. "I didn't realize I know one of the building's owners, that's all." She stepped toward the door as he re-opened it.

The sound of soft classical music filled the sparsely decorated lobby, and they headed for the brushed silver elevator doors. Ivy walked stiffly across the marble floor as her head swung from left to right, peering around as if expecting someone to pop out of the woodwork.

"The restaurant is on the top floor," he said, and pressed the button. "Are you all right?"

"Fine. Why?" She leaned left to look around the corner, then up at the number above the elevator door.

"Because you look like a criminal returning to the scene of a crime." He half laughed, wondering if he'd made a mistake.

The elevator dinged and she practically jumped inside without looking to see if it was even empty. He followed her inside, watching warily as she pushed the number 6 then the door close button.

Her shoulders lowered as the door closed, and she finally made eye contact with him. Any concern he had about her being a potential criminal fled when he saw the shimmer of frightened tears. Her chest rose and fell rapidly, and her hands knotted in the bottom of her shirt.

"Hey," he said softly and pressed the stop button. "What just happened?" He stepped closer and slid his hands over hers. Her jaw clenched but she released her shirt to take his hands. He pressed hers between his palms to stop them from shaking. "What am I missing?"

"Nothing." She closed her eyes for a moment and when she reopened them anger flashed through the tears lining her lower lashes. "Wesley Matrone is my ex-boyfriend."

"He owns the building?" Zane frowned.

"Apparently." She shook her head and pulled a hand back to swipe at her eyes. "I moved here after I got away from him."

Her words made him tense all over. "Did he hurt you?" he asked roughly.

"Not physically. That's why he's not in jail." Her tone was icy. "Well, that, and a good attorney." She blew out a breath and squeezed his hand. "Just so you know; I'm not scared. I mean, I was. Now I'm mad." She huffed a small laugh. "Unfortunately, I cry when I'm mad."

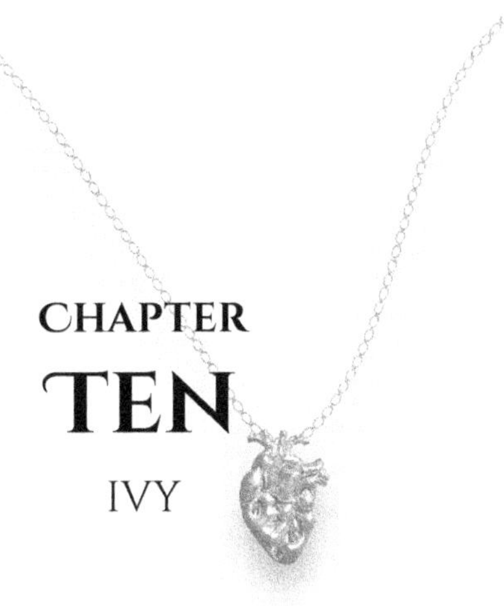

CHAPTER
TEN

IVY

Ivy hated the fact that just the sight of Wes's name could make her cry, but she blew out slow breath as Zane thumbed the stupid tears from her cheek. His brown eyes were dark as they searched hers. He looked ready to fight, and every nerve in her body responded to how close he was standing. She stared at the feather of muscle in his cheek as his jaw flexed repeatedly.

"If you want to go somewhere else — "he started.

"I don't," she said firmly. "I won't let him intimidate me anymore."

Wes controlled her life for two years. She left upstate and moved here to prove she wouldn't give him anymore of her life. More angry tears pooled but didn't fall. All it took was seeing his name, and she voluntarily handed him five more minutes. He wasn't getting any more.

Zane watched her, and a smile curved his lip. He shook his head slowly as the darkness in his eyes shifted from anger to respect to something that made her stomach quiver.

"Are you sure?" he asked. "You don't need to prove anything."

She squared her shoulders and took in the gorgeous man in front of her. "I am, and I'm sorry for — "

"Don't you dare apologize." His tone was soft but fierce as he pressed the button to start the elevator moving again. A twitch of amusement flared in his expression. "There's a favorite saying at the theater when it's show time, but emotions are high and tears are involved." He inched closer, and she held her breath. "Mascara is waterproof, the stage is solid, and the crowd is waiting."

"What does that mean?" she asked breathlessly. His nearness set off all kinds of fluttering in her chest and stomach, as if their closeness generated some strange electrical connection.

He touched the corner of her eye, wiping away a streak of makeup. "It means, you look amazing, you're not going to die, and there are people who want to see you succeed." He waved a hand. "Loosely translated anyway."

The door opened, and she sucked in a tiny breath. She forced herself not to look past him, though Zane's face blurred as a tendril of fear gripped her chest again. The chances of Wes being here had to be slim to none, but her mind screamed that he was waiting just outside the open elevator.

A shift in the air sent a whiff of Zane's cologne to her as he continued to block her line of sight, and for a split second, a different kind of panic hit her. What would Wes say about Zane and the way he dressed? She opened her mouth to ask if they could eat somewhere else, until she realized what an insult that would be to Zane.

She just told him she wasn't going to let Wes intimidate her, yet here she was, worried Wes's opinions. Zane would think she was ashamed to be seen with him. She wasn't. He was the kind of man she wanted to be with no matter what anyone thought of him.

Zane watched her, probably expecting her to change her mind, but she squared her shoulders and offered what she hoped was a confident smile. His expression softened and he offered his hand.

"Ready?"

"Yes." She sighed when he wove their fingers together.

He turned, and they stepped into an elegant foyer. To their left, a low rail of black metal topped with wood separated the entryway from a large dining room mostly filled with patrons. The clinking sound of plates and silverware carried over the classical music and hum of conversation, and the smell of steak drifted from the open kitchen window at the back of the room.

This was exactly the kind of place Wes would frequent if he were in town, and she couldn't stop herself from scanning the room for him. She clenched her jaw as frustration welled, threatening to make her cry again. Willing her shoulders to relax, she focused on the reality that she was having dinner with Zane Parish and dropped her gaze to their intertwined fingers. Zane's tightened slightly as if to let her know he wasn't rushing her.

She lifted her eyes to his, and another flash of inexplicable understanding flashed between them. Without breaking eye contact, he lifted the back of her hand to his lips, sending a shower of sparks up her arm and igniting a flash of desire in the deep brown of his irises. She drew a shaky breath as he lowered their hands.

"There's a ladies room right outside the restaurant if you need a minute." She blinked at him, and he shrugged slightly. "I work with mostly women. You lot tend not to believe us when we tell you that you look amazing, or that your mascara really is waterproof." He nodded toward the appropriate door. "Go see for yourself. I'll let the maitre'd know we're here."

CHAPTER

ELEVEN

ZANE

Zane watched Ivy until she disappeared inside the ladies room. She was clearly terrified of this Wesley guy. He had no idea if the man had legitimately done anything to make her feel that way, but he now had a good reason to ask Dani and Baden to check her out. He headed for the maitre'd and palmed his phone from his pocket.

> Z: I know you've probably already done it, but would you look into Ivy for me?

Dani replied instantly.

> D: I wouldn't do that without your permission. We're on it. Give us 10 minutes.

> Z: No hurry. Tomorrow is fine.

He slipped the phone back in his pocket and confirmed their seating reservation. Seconds later, his phone buzzed. Dani had sent a picture, and it made his neck tighten.

The photo looked like it had been taken on the red carpet of some fancy real estate publicity event. Ivy stood next to a tall, blond man in a tux, her blue formal dress pooling around her like a waterfall. But this wasn't the soft, playful Ivy he knew. He zoomed in on her face and frowned. Heavy makeup hid the naturally rosy glow of her cheeks, and the dark shadow and liner stole all the vibrance from her colorful eyes. But as he studied the photo, he realized it wasn't the makeup that made her look flat and dull. There was a hollowness in her expression that chilled him. It was as if she was nothing but a beautiful shell standing beside the widely grinning man.

He thumbed the picture to get a better look at the guy, then nearly dropped his phone when Ivy touched his arm.

"Is everything okay?" she asked.

He guiltily blacked the screen and put the phone away. "Yeah. It was just a message from my sister."

"Thank you for giving me a minute. I don't usually flake out like that, I promise." Her relaxed expression eased his concern.

He glanced toward the hostess who gestured for them to follow her. He offered Ivy his arm when she nodded. "You didn't flake out." He covered her hand with his, then flinched when she pinched his forearm. "Ham and potatoes!" he cursed. "What was that for?"

Her laugh was like music. "I'm just making sure this isn't a dream." Her cheeks pinked with the glow missing from her picture, fanning his flirtatious side.

He bent and whispered in her ear, "Aren't you supposed to ask me to pinch you?"

In response, she ducked her chin and leaned closer to him. "Seemed a bit forward to ask that on a first date." The green in her eyes danced like leaves in the wind when her gaze met his. "Maybe the second?" The vulnerability of the question in her expression did him in.

"Okay. I see the progression here." He raised a mocking brow. "First you pinch me, then I return the favor. I'm not the kind of guy who goes all the way after two dates. I prefer to wait until at least the third or fourth. Unless you don't want to see me more than twice?"

he taunted. She pinched him again, a little harder. "Son of a tomato pie!" he exclaimed.

Ivy burst out laughing, and several restaurant patrons looked up in surprise.

"Stop that," he chided, and Ivy stifled her giggles as a few of the patrons gave them stern looks.

"I wanted to hear you curse again," she said. "Do you always curse with food?"

The hostess stopped at a table near the back corner of the restaurant and placed the menus upright at their seats before retreating.

"It's a habit I picked up from my dad." He held Ivy's seat as she sat, then took his across from her. "Mom hated it when he cursed in front of us kids, but he wasn't one to hold back." He pointed to the menu. "Order whatever looks good."

"I might have to try that."

Her voice trailed off as she scanned the menu, and he waited for her to react to the prices. When her wide eyes met his, he nodded. "I promise can afford it. Get whatever you like."

Another flicker of doubt played across her face but cleared as quickly as it came. "I haven't had lobster in forever. Is that okay?"

"If that's what you want," he said and glanced at his menu. "I was planning to get the steak. Together, we'll be surf and turf."

"Okay, that's totally cheesy." She scolded, but the sparkle in her eyes was worth it. "How many siblings do you have?"

He took a quick drink of water to buy himself a second. "There are seventeen of us," he said and watched her face. She didn't flinch.

"My mom comes from a big family, too. I think she has six brothers and two sisters. We don't see them very often so it's hard to keep track." She studied him. "Are you close to yours?"

He chuckled, remembering Dani's raid on his closet hours earlier. "Closer than we should be sometimes. My sister and brother-in-law are also in Arena; the rest of the family get together a couple times a year."

She leaned forward, all the fear and anger completely gone from her expression. "I bet it's a lot of fun. I always wanted a brother or a sister, but I ended up being an only child."

It actually made him nervous that she didn't react at all. In a few days, this girl had not only captured his attention with little effort, but she'd accepted his style and his unusual family size without question. Suddenly, he not only wanted to know her better, but he wanted to let her into his everyday life. Something he'd never done. The idea warmed his skin, and he wondered if she knew how to play Euchre.

"Earth to Zane." She angled her head into his line of sight, and he realized he'd been staring at nothing. "Where did you just go?"

He refocused on her soft features, and hoped his skin wasn't as red as it felt. "I was thinking about how beautiful you are," he said and meant it.

Her neck flushed, and she tucked a lock of hair behind her ear. "Thank you. That means a lot coming from you." She glanced up as the waiter brought their salads. "You spend a lot of time with women much prettier than me."

Just like that, she reminded him of the other reason he preferred not to date. Women were always comparing themselves to the models, dancers, and actresses he worked with. They were the faces of his co-workers, and none of them had ever crossed into his personal life. Yet, the few girls he dated chose not to believe that was even possible when what they saw on screen or stage was edited and airbrushed to perfection.

"That comment took longer than I expected." He picked up his fork and speared a tomato. "First of all, makeup and camera angles can do wonders. Second, it's a job I do because I enjoy dancing." He really hoped she understood. "What you see as the final cut isn't nearly as sexy and sensuous as it seems. True romance doesn't happen on a movie set when there are thirty people watching and analyzing every move, every angle." He rarely watched a finished video project anymore. It wasn't reality, and when girls had begun expecting him to behave like the characters he portrayed, he'd nearly stopped accepting job offers. Thankfully, his agent talked him out of it. "I get paid well for acting like I'm into the women I dance with, but it's just that, an act. Nothing more."

"Hey," she interrupted softly, almost shyly, and he realized he'd responded more harshly than intended. "I'm not accusing you of anything." She surprised him again with her next words. "I've only known you a few days, and I already know you're not that guy. It's hard not to wonder though. You've been on screen with some pretty big names."

"And big egos to match." He sighed. "I guess it's my turn to apologize. My career has been an issue before, and I guess I hoped…" He paused considering how much it would reveal so soon, but she saved him the trouble.

"I don't want it to be an issue either. I didn't mean to make it one."

The pressure in his chest eased. "You didn't make it anything. I'm the one who overreacted."

She shook her head with a wry smile. "We're a mess of issues, aren't we?"

"Eh. Everyone has something, right?"

She nodded and they tucked into their food, chatting casually and laughing until the waiter cleared their entrée plates and promised desert would be out shortly.

Ivy sighed and leaned forward, resting her hand beside her empty water glass. He slid his fingers over hers.

"Thank you for having dinner with me tonight." He glanced at their hands when she wove their fingers together. "I'd really like to do it again."

"Me too." She seemed about to say something else, but her gaze snagged on something behind him, and she tugged his hand as alarm spread across her face. "We should go."

Zane rose with her but before he could ask what was wrong, a deep voice sent chills up his back.

"Playing for the other team now, sweetheart?" Ivy's alarm shifted to terror, then rage as the man continued. "Being with a man like me must have ruined you."

"Let's go." She gave Zane pleading look and squeezed his hand when he started to turn. "Don't give him the satisfaction."

Zane couldn't leave the man at his back. Instinctively positioning Ivy behind him, he turned and took in the man who had to be Wes. Tall and clean cut, he wore what looked like an expensively tailored suit. His dark eyes landed on Zane and his lip curled as his eyes slid down then back up to study Zane's face.

"What are you?" he sneered.

"Comfortable." Zane replied and held out a hand. "I'm Zane Parish."

The man ignored him and flicked his gaze up and down Ivy. He rocked back in obvious disgust and waved a hand in her direction. "Is that outfit a joke?"

"No, but your attitude has to be." Zane kept his tone light, hoping to break the tension, but when the man's gaze hardened, he squared his shoulders and shifted forward. "I know you didn't mean to insult her."

"The only insult is that she left me for...whatever you are."

The man had at least thirty pounds on him, and Zane wasn't a fighter, but that didn't keep his free hand from clenching into a fist. The man noticed and lowered his chin.

"Go ahead," he taunted.

Ivy's hand trembled in his, and she attempted to step between them, but Zane stopped her.

"I think we're done here." Zane extended a hand one more time. "It was nice meeting you."

"You have no idea who I am, do you?" Wes sneered.

"I know enough." Zane said firmly and didn't flinch when the man stepped into his space. They were the same height, and Zane met him glare for glare until something made the man take a step back. Devon's low, Creole accent made Zane smirk.

"Is this man disturbing you, Mr. Parish?" The restaurant owner easily matched Wes in size, and the way he moved and handled himself made it clear he was no one to mess with.

"No. We were just introducing ourselves." Zane made sure to stay in Wes's line of sight, keeping him from intimidating Ivy and subtly letting Devon know what the real concern was. "I don't think I caught your name."

"Wesley Matrone." The man shifted onto his heels, though the threat in his eyes didn't retreat with him. "I recently purchased this…"

"I apologize for not recognizing you, Mr. Matrone." Devon interrupted with false deference. "I was told you would be dining with the other partners tonight." When Wes ignored him and slid his glare slid toward Ivy, Devon moved to stand shoulder to shoulder with Zane, effectively shielding her behind them. "I would be happy to give you a tour of the restaurant and show you to your table."

"I would appreciate that." Wes forced a smile that was more of a smirk, making it clear he was only backing down to prevent a scene. "I don't want to keep the others waiting."

Zane glanced behind him to make sure Ivy was all right. Other than the glitter of angry tears, she looked as ready to fight as he and Devon.

"This way." Devon stepped forward, indicating a glass enclosed room a few yards away. With a last glare, Wes turned on his heel and followed the restaurant owner.

CHAPTER

TWELVE

IVY

Ivy couldn't speak as Zane guided her out of the restaurant and into the elevator. Had that really just happened? She swallowed and risked a glance at Zane. He stared intently at the number above the door as if willing the machine to hurry. She bit the inside of her cheek to hold back the frustrated tears. In ten minutes, Wes had ruined her life again. Her chest hitched involuntarily, and Zane's hand tightened on hers.

"One more floor." His voice strained. "Devon won't let him follow us."

She couldn't stop the shaking in her arms as they exited the building. "I'm so sorry," she said miserably.

"No." He stepped in front of her gently lifted her chin. "You have no reason to apologize for that son of a..." He clamped his mouth closed and exhaled through his nose. The pad of his thumb brushed the lower edge of her lip as he stroked her chin then dropped his hand. "That was not your fault."

She expected to see wariness or disgust, but he looked at her with concern and a flicker of something that made her stomach flip. "Thank you for what you and Devon did." She dropped her gaze, not wanting him to see her crying again, but when his arms went around her and he tucked her close, she couldn't stop the strangled sob that escaped. Thankfully, she held herself mostly together and didn't totally break down. The surprising strength gained from being in Zane's arms enabled her to gather her emotions, and she loosened her grip on his back. He didn't let her go far.

"Are you okay to walk back, or do you want me to call us a cab?" His hands cupped her shoulders as she took a small step away.

"I can walk." After Wes's appearance, it might be the last few minutes she had with him. "It's not far."

He slid his palm down her arm and recaptured her fingers. They walked half a block in silence before he cleared his throat.

"Would it be too much to ask what happened between the two of you?" he asked.

Ivy's mind flashed back to the day that had convinced her to leave Wes. She was proud when her voice didn't break, though the terror she'd felt that night made her whole body tremble. "For the two years I lived with him, he controlled everything, and I let him. Until he smashed the key-fob to my car when I came home late wearing an outfit he hadn't pre-approved before I left his condo." Zane stiffened and she felt him staring at her profile. "It wasn't the first time he got violent, but until that night I never thought he would direct it at me." She ground her teeth. "All I did was go visit my parents, but for the rest of the night he grilled me about where I was and who was with me. He called my parents and talked to them but still accused me of lying." The sound of plastic shattering and the thud of his high-priced shoe on the kitchen floor still echoed through her head. "I waited until he was at work, and I ran to a friend's house. I stayed with her for a few days, then moved here. I work as a virtual assistant, so it was easy to hide for a while." Her apartment building came in sight, and she wondered if she was going to have to move again. "But I always knew he would find me. That's why I have the dog. He's a pet, but he's also trained to protect me."

Zane slowed his pace. "Do you have a protection order in place?"

"I do, but unless he physically attacks me, it's not much more than a paper trail. It won't keep him from stalking me." She glanced toward the restaurant. "Or moving into any neighborhood I try to run to."

"Your management company is aware?" he asked. "They have 24-hour surveillance and a security patrol?"

"Yes. They know, and I moved here because their security is so tight." She looked up when he relaxed a fraction.

"Good. Then I don't need to worry about making any calls." He flashed her a smile when she stopped and stared. "What? Did you think I'd let that continue?"

"I...I don't know what to think." She stammered.

"Well..." His gaze slid over her face like a caress. "I think you should have dinner with me again."

"You do?"

His laugh made her skin tingle. "Yes. Are you busy Friday?"

"No." She let him draw her forward again. They were less than a block from her apartment. "Are you sure?"

His hand tightened on hers. "Very sure. I haven't cooked in a long time. Would you be all right if I invited you to eat at my place? No chance we'll be interrupted there."

"You cook?"

"I'm a great cook actually. At least Dani and Zach never complained when we lived together." He touched his chest. "I make a pretty decent hardboiled egg."

The tension of the night shattered as she couldn't hold back a laugh. "You boil water?"

He gave her an indignant look, but the satisfied gleam in his eye told her he meant to make her laugh. "Not everyone can." He nodded to her building. "503, right?"

"Yes." She tugged her keys from her purse.

A cool breeze filled her nose with Zane's cologne, and his thumb caressed the back of her hand as they climbed the steps to her door.

Tofu barked once and his white muzzle poked through the mail slot. Seemingly satisfied it was her, he withdrew, and his nails stilled on the tile.

Zane's amused expression made her heart flutter, and when his gorgeous eyes met hers, she couldn't look away.

"Thank you for walking me home," she managed.

"It's a beautiful night," he said and edged closer. Ivy tilted her chin to maintain eye contact. "And I kind of liked the company."

She laughed nervously. "Me too."

He touched her cheek and leaned forward. She closed her eyes and waited for his lips to brush hers but sucked in a little gasp of surprise when his breath warmed her forehead instead. His kiss brushed the skin above her eye.

"Good night, Ivy," he said and stepped back. "I'm looking forward to cooking dinner for you Friday."

Embarrassment and disappointment flushed her cheeks, and she fought to keep her voice steady. "So am I."

She pushed the door open, planning to slip inside and disappear, but he stopped her with a light tug on her hand. She told herself he wouldn't notice the tears, but when his expression softened, she dropped her gaze.

His fingers tightened and he lifted her hand to his lips. "Friday?"

Unwilling to trust her voice, she nodded and smiled weakly as he let go and moved down a step.

"Go on inside. I want to know the door is locked before I leave." He tucked his hands in his pockets and nodded to the partially open door.

"Thank you," she said quietly and slid inside.

Once the door was closed and locked, she peered through the peephole and watched him lift the hem of his skirt, jog down the stairs, and stride away.

Tofu nudged her leg with a whine.

"I don't know, buddy." She scratched his head absently. "I really thought…" what? That after meeting and defending them both from her psyho ex-boyfriend he would want to kiss her? She rolled her eyes and dropped to a knee to embrace Tofu's neck. He laid his chin on her shoulder and licked her cheek.

"I think there's some ice cream still in the freezer." She rose and headed for the kitchen. "Want to share?"

Tofu's answering howl made her smile.

THIRTEEN

ZANE

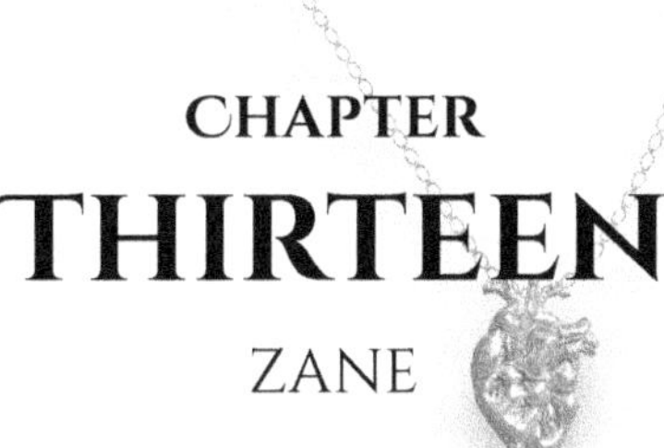

Zane removed the strip of foil from the edge of the casserole and cursed when he burned his fingers. He lowered the oven temperature and gave the sauce a stir as Apple landed gracefully on the counter.

"Not tonight." He lifted her and scratched her head before setting her back on the floor. She mewed in protest and tried to jump onto the counter again. "We have a guest coming, and she might not appreciate your paw prints in her dinner." The cat sat and licked her chest as if she didn't care one way or the other, but he knew better. "I'm not leaving the kitchen, so you might as well go sulk somewhere else." She yawned and rolled to her back in the middle of the floor. He shook his head, and the thought struck him that Ivy might not even like cats. She had a big dog. What if she was allergic?

He glanced toward the bedroom. Should he lock Apple up? The cat stalked toward the cabinets again.

"Whether she likes cats or not, you aren't listening, so away you go." He scooped her up as he tried to dart past him. She rubbed her head under his chin as he carried her to his room. "I'm sorry, girl." He deposited her on the bed and closed the door. "Sweet bean burrito, the casserole!"

The front door opened then closed solidly as he hurried back to the kitchen and reached for the pan, burning the rest of his fingers. "Sausage links and donuts!" he cursed and swiped the oven mitt from the open drawer beside him.

"That smells amazing, but your language is out of control, Z," his sister called.

"Stuff it, Dani. I'm already running late." He double checked the temperature, then slid the pan back into the oven. He straightened and closed the oven door, glaring at his sister. She leaned against the frame, positively enjoying every moment of his nervousness. "Remind me again why I asked you to stop by?"

"Because you are so bewitched by this girl that you forgot these?" She pulled a bouquet of flowers from behind her back and headed for the sink where he already had a vase waiting.

"I didn't forget," he snapped back. "I ran out of time. Who knew the bakery and the florist closed at 5?"

He tossed his oven mitts on top of the stove, then snatched them back before they caught fire on the burner heating the sauce.

Dani said nothing, though her brows went up. She neatly trimmed the stems, and he watched as she dropped them in the vase. She chuckled again when he moved her out of the way to re-arrange them.

"You really are nervous," she said quietly.

He turned the vase to survey the blooms, then raked a hand through his hair. "She's the first girl I've ever brought here."

Dani's hands stilled from cleaning up the trimmed stems. "I didn't know." Her tone almost sounded hurt. "You never told me that."

He leaned on the counter. "I don't tell you everything, you know." He waited for her to make a snide remark, but she picked up the vase and carried it to the dining room to set it in the center of the table.

He followed and waited for her to comment on the new china and table linens, but she was quiet as she rested a hand on the back of a chair. Her approving smile widened when she met his gaze.

"This is all new?" Her smile turned knowing when he nodded. "You've never tried this hard to impress a girl."

He ignored the heat at the back of his neck and shrugged. "I never had to. Ivy's different. Special." He shook his head slightly. "I don't know what I'm doing."

Dani gestured to the table. "I think you know exactly what you're doing, but okay." She paused and her eyes widened. "Wait. Are you planning to..." She glanced toward the closed bedroom door.

"No. No!" He barely remembered not to crush his palms against his face and ruin his makeup. "Is that what this will look like to her?" Horror washed over him. Would she really think he invited her to his house so he could sleep with her? "We haven't even...after dinner the other night I didn't..." He dropped his eyes.

"Wait. Have you kissed her?" she asked in surprise and covered her mouth when his face flushed. "No?"

"I haven't." He bit his lip.

"Why?" She blinked and amended. "Not that it's any of my business, but...I thought you really liked her."

"That's why." He exhaled when she looked confused. "When you kissed Baden the first time it changed everything for you."

"Z...It's different for us. You can't compare a blood bonding kiss to..." she said, but he raised a hand to stop her.

"I know, and that's not what I meant." His voice shook and he turned away to hide his frustration. "But that doesn't mean my first kiss with Ivy can't be just as special." He straightened a place mat. "It might not bond us like it did you and Baden, but it could be the start of something...permanent." His heart kicked up remembering how badly he'd wanted to taste her lips while standing her front steps, and how hard it had been to leave after seeing the disappointment in her eyes when she realized he wasn't going to. "I couldn't do it after the awful dinner the other night. I didn't want our first kiss associated with drama from her ex."

Dani's sniff brought his head around. She never cried, and the sight of her tears was like a kick to the stomach. She was going to tell him he was wrong, that he should have kissed her. The look on Ivy's face was his clue. Kissing her would have been a better ending to her stressful night, but he had walked away. He was an idiot.

"I messed up, didn't I?" He shoved his hands in his pockets and stared at the ceiling.

She crossed the room and cupped his face in her hands, forcing him to look at her. "You didn't mess up. Not even close." She patted his cheek. "Dad would be proud of you." Her broken whisper made him suck in a breath, and he pulled her against him.

"Thank you, sis. That means a lot."

She squeezed him, then let go. "She's a lucky girl." The clock in the hall struck the half hour, and she glanced at her watch. "I should go in case she's early."

He walked her to the door, obsessively adjusting random items as they went. Dani looked at him sideways, then sighed.

"I guess I should tell you Baden looked into her story." She kept walking when he froze, his stomach knotting. He'd almost forgotten, and he wasn't sure he wanted to know, but the unasked question hung between them until he couldn't stand it.

"What did he find out?"

She opened the door and paused on the top step. When she turned and gave him a long look, his heart sank. "Be careful with her."

He swallowed as the knot in his stomach twisted. "Why?" he asked cooly.

"Because her story checks out," Dani said quietly. "That guy, Wes, basically held her hostage for almost a year." She searched his face, but he kept his fury in check. Apparently satisfied with what she saw and probably scented from him; she nodded. "You did the right thing by waiting." He blew out the breath he'd been holding. "You both deserve a fresh start." She stepped onto the landing and gave him a wicked smile. "Be warned though. That forever kiss...it packs a punch."

FOURTEEN

Ivy punched in the code Zane sent her and parked in the visitor section of the garage. His sixth-floor condo was in the wide building encased in glass and steel attached to the parking garage. One of her clients lived here, and the mortgage payments she made for him were more than her annual salary.

She sat in the car and stared at her phone as a wave of deja vu crested over her. Though the building in front of her looked nothing like the one she and Wes lived in, Zane's wealth and status finally struck her. He told her to dress casually, but though they were name brand, her second-hand comfortable jeans and favorite embroidered tunic suddenly felt cheap and out of fashion. Flipping the visor mirror revealed her nerves had splotched her cheeks and neck with red patches, and her eyeliner was uneven. Wes would be annoyed.

The phone vibrated in her hand, making her jump. It was a text message from Zane.

Z - Did you find the garage? Turn left when you get off the elevator. The door is unlocked.

For a moment she considered telling him she couldn't find it, and reached for the ignition, but her phone buzzed again. This time he called.

"Hi. I'm not sure where I'm supposed to park," she hedged.

"Anywhere is fine." He chuckled. "I called because I was afraid I gave you the wrong code, but it looks like I got it right. I've never given it to anyone before, and I forgot the system notifies me when a guest uses it."

Her neck tightened, and she leaned forward, peering into the shadowed corners of the garage for cameras.

"Can you see where I am?" she asked.

"No. It just tells me when someone uses my code." His voice dropped. "Are you all right? I can come down to meet you."

She let out a quiet breath and cursed herself for being ridiculous. *He's not Wes.*

"Ivy?" he said.

"You don't need to come down." She reached for the door handle. "I can see the elevator from here. I'll be there in a minute."

"Take your time," he said, and she closed her eyes at his sincerity. "I'll meet you on the second floor. And Ivy?"

"Yeah?"

"Do you happen to like cats?"

The question was so unexpected she paused with her purse halfway up her arm. "Yes, why?"

"Just curious." The smile in his voice warmed her skin. "I'll see you in a minute."

She locked up the car and headed for the elevator, trying to hold back a silly grin. Did he really have cats, or was he trying to ease her mind? It was very like him to say something just to make her smile.

She pressed the up button on the elevator, but nothing happened. She pressed it again, then noticed the keypad below it and tried the code he'd given her to get into the garage. The buttons lit up and the door slid open as her phone buzzed again.

"Impatient much?" She teased.

"A little." Zane said sheepishly. "I forgot to tell you the elevator uses the same code, but it looks like you figured that out too. I'll be right outside the door."

He sounded as nervous as she felt, which made her feel like a girl going on her first date. She tried to use the polished metal doors as a mirror but scowled when the slightly warped reflection did her no favors. The doors opened on the second floor, and she spotted Zane. His long strides slowed when he saw her. He wore a pair of over washed, ripped jeans and an untucked, blue plaid button up shirt. His gorgeous eyes flicked over her and he smiled.

"You found me," he said, and offered his hand as she stepped out of the elevator.

"A place like this is hard to miss," she breathed.

"Perks of the job." He laced his fingers through hers.

To her left, the hallway wall stretched toward another set of elevators, but the view to her right drew her eyes toward the rapidly coloring sky. The entire outside wall of the building was glass. He slowed with her as she marveled at the view.

He led her past an elegant seating area with caramel leather couches and a beautiful view of the river beyond the city park. He must have caught her staring and squeezed her hand.

"The view is the same from my living room."

He pushed open a nondescript door and gestured for her to precede him inside. The entryway opened into a wide great room filled with the scent of Mexican spices and cooked beef. A dining table set with sparkling white plates and colorfully striped napkins was set for two, and a low vase of flowers sat in the center. Beyond the table, his navy, leather living room furniture gleamed with oranges and yellows from the setting sun washing the room in warm light. The view made her breath catch, and she crossed the room to stand in front of the wall of glass. The windows of his condo wrapped around the corner of the building, giving her a 180-degree view of the town below.

Zane appeared beside her and offered a glass of wine.

"I can close the blinds if the view is too distracting," he said.

Ivy could just make out the bike path she and Tofu walked every day as she took the glass from him without looking.

"Distracting?"

"Yes," he chuckled and gestured out the window. "I can't compete with that."

"I thought this was why you invited me." She sipped the wine and pointedly didn't look his way, though she watched his reflection in the glass. "For the view, I mean."

His eyes caught hers in the reflection. "Of course I did. I'm glad you like it." He focused past her. "It's one of the reasons I moved here. It gives me perspective."

"How so?" Ivy turned and took in the rest of the room. Built in bookshelves stretched along one wall, broken by a large flat screen TV and sleek entertainment system. An opening in the wall on the opposite side of the room passed through into the kitchen and the doorway spilled white light onto the gray carpeting of a hall that must lead to the bedrooms.

"It reminds me that I control my life not the other way around." He shrugged. "My schedule can get a little crazy but coming home and looking at that makes me feel a little less claustrophobic."

She glanced over her shoulder and then back at him. The sunset had faded to mostly gray in a few minutes, but the warmth missing from the sky was replaced by the open way he watched her.

His gaze flicked across her face, and she realized he wore only minimal makeup. Liner edged his lashes, but even without the contouring and gold shadow his natural masculine structure still made her belly flip.

"I apologize if I seem a bit nervous. The only people who've ever been here are my brothers and sister," he said softly.

He was nervous? It struck her then, and all the nerves inside her unwound with the impact of what he'd done. He was showing her his behind the scenes. This was his sanctuary away from the cameras and the pressure of being a performer. He'd let his guard down for her.

"Thank you for letting me in," she said. "It's beautiful."

"So are you." He looked away almost shyly. "Are you hungry?"

"I am. Whatever you made smells wonderful."

They crossed to the kitchen which gleamed with polished stainless steel and stone counters. He handed her a potholder and gestured to a small pot with a spoon in it as he bent to open the oven door.

"Do you mind carrying the sauce?"

"Nope." Ivy followed him back to the dining table hardly believing the night was happening until sense of deja vu made her pause.

The condo's layout suddenly struck her, and she swept her gaze toward the kitchen, then the bookcases and giant tv. She swallowed as a twinge of unease crept up her neck. The decorations and furniture were all very different, but the floor plan was exactly the same as the one Wes had been living in when they first met.

She set the pot on a trivet and gripped the back of the chair as Zane crossed the room and disappeared back into the kitchen. She dropped her chin and tried to ignore the way her chest tightened. Wes's voice whispered at the back of her mind as

"The rest of my guests will be here any minute." His sharp eyes raked over her. "That dress compliments your coloring, but it looks rumpled unless you stand up straight. Don't slouch."

She lifted her shoulders and dropped her hands from the back of the chair, then jumped when Zane touched her arm. His concerned expression made her blow out a slow breath.

"They're just enchiladas. They won't bite." His mouth tipped up. "Where did you just go?"

"No where." How could she possibly explain that simply being in his apartment reminded her of Wes? Thankfully, she didn't have to force her smile when Zane's thumb stroked the back of her hand. "It's still hard sometimes..." she trailed off, not sure how to explain.

"Anything can be a trigger." he said.

Shame prickled the back of her neck. How did he know? She dropped her gaze then shivered when his fingers gently lifted her chin.

"I get it." He glanced at the glass wall behind her and then ticked his head toward the front door. "You already know that view comes with a lot of security." He fixed his chocolate brown eyes on hers. "I was attacked in my own home once, so I know what it's like to be afraid."

It took a second for the implications of what he said to sink in. She forgot about Wes and the words were out before she could think to stop them.

"Someone attacked you? Here?" She bit her lip when he focused past her, and when he seemed to be considering saying anything more she stepped back. "I'm sorry. I shouldn't have — "

"Don't apologize. It happened long before I moved here." His fingers tightened before he let go and pulled out a chair for her. "Unfortunately, I learned the hard way what could happen if I allowed strangers to know where I actually live."

He took the seat across from her and lifted the lid on the casserole. Her mouth watered as the room filled with the scent of onions and peppers, but something in his tone changed, drawing her attention completely to him.

"It happened right after my first big video hit the charts." His neck darkened, and anger flashed in his eyes. "No matter what it looks like on screen, I don't sleep around. A girl I dated a couple times interpreted my celibacy to mean I wasn't truly interested in women, and she sent one of her guy friends my way." He swallowed and his voice dropped even lower. "He didn't like taking no for an answer and was waiting for me at the farm late one night." Her stomach rolled, but he shook his head. "Thanks to my sister, it wasn't as bad as it could have been."

"Is this when you were living with her?"

"Yes. You have a good memory." He held out his hand for her

plate. "Dani, Zachary, and I lived at the homestead for a while." He scooped out a steaming enchilada. "Dani works from home and was up working on a job when the guy cornered me on the porch. She called the police and managed to film the whole thing. He was convicted of assault and trespassing and went to jail for a couple weeks, I think. Being in tight corners or confined spaces catches me off guard now and then, and I probably get the same look on my face you had a moment ago."

She took the plate as he searched her face. Whatever he saw there made him drop his gaze. Had Wes's threats been a trigger? The thought made her set the plate down harder than intended.

"I promise it does get better." He said and then indicated the pot she'd carried in. "The sauce is authentic. One of my sisters-in-law is Mexican. She taught me to cook."

The rich scent of the sauce barely registered as she lifted the lid. At least his family knew it wasn't his fault. Hers still believed Wes deserved another chance. She studied Zane's face, imagining how they would react to him. The moment they learned who he was, Wes would be forgotten, and the whole incident blamed on her fickleness. She let out a quiet breath of annoyance.

"*Your* family sounds wonderful," she said and winced at what that implied about hers. I was partially her fault. Until she escaped Wes, they hadn't known because she was too ashamed to tell them.

He gave her a curious look, then chuckled. "They have their moments. I would have given up if it weren't for their support. I let that guy get to me for a while." His gaze flicked away then back as he plated his own food. "I know how easy it is to blame yourself for letting things happen."

She stared. Did he really understand her that well?

"I believed the people who told me I brought the attack on myself because of my profession and the way I dressed. I stopped wearing the clothes I liked and quit using makeup. I even considered giving up dancing. I was afraid to be myself for almost a year, until Dani and my director at the theater finally staged an intervention.

The troop refused to let me quit, and my director took me to Brandon's store and put me in charge of ordering all the makeup. Dani restocked my closet and taught me to thrift shop while Alana taught me to cook." His expression grew rueful. "Someone offered to teach me self-defense, but I'm not a fighter. I am glad Devon was there, or I might have tried to take a swing."

Wes wasn't a fighter either, but she knew better than most what damage his words could do. Her hand tightened on the fork. Wes's cutting remarks hadn't truly been aimed at Zane. He'd wanted Ivy to defuse the tension and prevent a scene by giving in and leaving with him instead of Zane. It was a nasty trick he'd successfully pulled off before. He would have ignored Zane if it weren't for her.

FIFTEEN

ZANE

Ivy was quiet for a long moment, and the moisture on her lower lids made him pause.

"I'm sorry Wes said those horrible things to you," she said.

He blinked in surprise. "Why are you apologizing for him?"

"He wouldn't have said anything to you if you weren't with me."

Her tone had an edge, and her frustrated tears told him she knew Wes had been baiting them both, but the sincerity in her apology tightened his jaw.

He set his fork aside and met her gaze levelly. "He's an arrogant jerk, and he isn't the first person to say things like that. He also won't be the last. He knew what he was doing, and he knew it would get to you. Don't let him, and whatever you do, don't make excuses for him." Ivy stared at him with wide eyes. He exhaled and eased back in his seat. "It bothers me to hear you apologizing for his bad behavior. That's like taking the blame on yourself all over again."

When she didn't say anything, Zane wanted to kick himself. This was supposed to be a relaxing dinner to get to know her better. Instead, he dumped his past on her and chastised her as if she were one of his students.

"You're right. I do that," she said slowly. Her stunned expression eased, replaced by a sheepish one. "I spent years making excuses for him, and I guess it became a habit."

"It's easy to do I suppose. But no matter where we are or what we're doing, if I'm being a jerk, call me on it. Don't make excuses for me." He cursed internally. *What makes you think she'll want to see you again, genius?* He nodded to the food growing cold. "They're better hot."

The night was not going according to plan. He paused with his fork halfway to his mouth when Ivy flinched.

"Ow! Carrots and fudge! That hurts." She rubbed her forearm, and he started to get up. Her lips pinched together to hold back what he thought was a grimace until he caught the sparkle of laughter in her eyes.

He sank back regarding her narrowly. "Did you just pinch yourself?"

She took a bite of her food. "Maybe."

"Why?" he asked slowly.

"Because you said I couldn't ask you to do it until the third or fourth date, and I had to know if this was real." She scooped another bite and shrugged. "Don't look at me like that." She dropped her gaze. "You're going to make me believe you actually want a third date."

He stared. *I want a million more dates with you.* She stared right back until both of them broke into a grin and her cheeks pinked.

"Keep it up and I'll have to pinch myself again," she continued. "And I'm not sure I got the cursing thing right."

"You didn't do too bad for your first time," he said. "But carrots and fudge don't go together."

"I'll try to remember that." She smirked and pointed to her plate. "These are really good."

"Thank you."

They ate for a few minutes in comfortable silence. He tried not to watch her while she ate, but he couldn't keep his eyes off her. If she noticed, she didn't seem to mind. Being with Ivy felt as natural as breathing, and his mind bounced in several directions at once.

Ivy truly saw him. Not his clothes, not his minor celebrity status, but who he was as a man. And she managed to draw out the most painful part of his past effortlessly. He had never told that story to anyone, yet he wanted to tell Ivy everything. The protective instincts that flared at the restaurant could easily turn to something deeper if he let them. The thought made him pause.

He glanced at the pictures of his brothers and sister tucked into his bookcases. There was no doubt his family would love her. Though the thought of Ivy and Dani together made him chuckle internally. They would be best friends or partners in crime. He wasn't sure which scenario would be better.

"Do you have a cat?" she asked suddenly.

"Huh?" He blinked.

"You asked me if I liked cats." She raised an eyebrow. "Was that a distraction or do you have one?"

He glanced at the slightly open bedroom door. "I do. Her name is Apple."

She raised a brow and set her fork on the empty plate. "Please don't tell me the food thing extends to naming kids and animals."

He laughed and pushed back from the table. "No. Her full name, however, is Burnt Apple Fritter. It was my dad's favorite curse. It seemed fitting for her."

"Oh. So, she's one of *those* cats." Ivy snorted.

"Not really."

She rose with him, and they cleared the table. He tucked the last dish into the dishwasher then turned to watch Ivy where she stood looking out the window.

"What are you thinking?" she asked, and their gazes connected in the glass.

He didn't answer right away. Instead, he picked up his phone, started some music, and flipped the tv to a screen saver that looked like a fireplace. She faced him, curiosity making her smile lopsided, and his stomach fluttered like it did before a live show.

She watched him warily as he extended a hand. Her chest hitched when he tucked his other hand behind his back and took a step toward her. "You wondered if I would want to dance with you." He turned her palm flat against his and gently pulled her forward until they were nearly touching. "I absolutely do."

He reached for her other hand and placed it on his shoulder then slid his arm loosely around her waist. Her cheeks were bright with color and the green in her eyes danced like falling leaves.

He moved closer, using their joined hands to guide her into a gliding step back then to the side. She looked down at their feet, and her brows drew close in concentration. He leaned forward to whisper in her ear.

"My eyes are up here." He couldn't resist glancing at her lips as she lifted her chin. When her eyes paused at his mouth before meeting his, he discovered he was suddenly and uncharacteristically nervous.

A long moment passed before she relaxed into the song's rhythm with him, and he moved closer until he could feel her warm, uneven breaths against his throat. The sensation sent shivers down his back, and he resisted a sigh as she slipped both hands up to rest her forearms on his shoulders. He clasped his wrists at the hollow of her back, savoring the way she felt in his arms.

"It's not so scary, is it?" He couldn't keep the roughness out of his voice, and his stomach tightened when her eyes darkened in response. "I would very much like to kiss you," he rasped.

The flash of mischief in her eyes sent his pulse rocketing.

"Was that a question or a statement?" she asked.

He leaned in, pausing when there was little more than a breath between them. "It was both."

A bolt of surprise rocked through him when she closed the distance a fraction more. Her lips were light as a feather as she whispered, "The answer is yes."

In no hurry, he drew back to take in the colors of her eyes and stifled a sigh as she moistened her lips. When her fingers grazed the back of his neck, encouraging him closer, he held her gaze until he lowered his mouth to hers.

Her lips were as soft as he'd expected, and she surprised him again by catching his lower lip between hers. Following her lead, he deepened the kiss for a moment, then eased away. His breath left him in a rush when her body relaxed, and she tucked her head under his chin. He held her, sliding his thumb back and forth across her spine as he led her in a slow dance around his living room.

He couldn't remember the last time he'd held a woman without feeling like she expected more than a simple dance. Ivy's hands trailed down his arms and he lifted his elbows to give her room to wrap her arms around his waist. She immediately settled against him as if she never planned to let go. He slipped a hand into the silky hair at the nape of her neck, and squeezed his eyes shut as he pressed his cheek to the top of her head. She fit perfectly in his arms, and though he didn't want to, he reluctantly lifted his head and loosened his hold as the song ended. She made an impatient noise and pressed her fingers into his back, refusing to let him move away. He answered by lowering his lips to the top of her head and blinked back the stinging in his eyes as a wave of contentment washed the last of the tension from his body.

As the second song ended, he lifted her chin and kissed her again, lingering, soft, and full of promises he couldn't speak yet. She responded, mirroring the angle of his mouth and the rhythm of his body as he continued to guide their dance over the floor, until she tensed and pulled back with a puff of surprised breath through her nose. He followed her gaze as she looked down and they both side-stepped, nearly tripping over Apple who had apparently escaped the bedroom to wind herself between Ivy's legs.

They giggled, and he ran a thumb across his lower lip as Ivy crouched down to pet the intruder.

"Ivy, meet Burnt Apple Fritter," he said wryly and dropped to a knee beside her.

"She's beautiful," Ivy murmured and ran a hand down the cat's arched back.

"So are you." He carefully reached out, turned Ivy's face to his, and brushed a kiss to her lips before rising to sit on the couch.

Ivy watched him as a blush colored her cheeks, then she snuggled in next to him as if she'd done it a thousand times. He wrapped an arm around her, tucking her close, and was completely unsurprised when Apple leapt gracefully into his lap and rubbed her head against Ivy's arm.

She laughed and met his eyes. "I think she likes me."

"She has good taste." He shifted to allow the cat to settle on his lap, but she stretched out, half on him and half on Ivy. He silently thanked her for staking the claim he couldn't yet. He didn't want Ivy to leave either. "And it also means you're our captive until she gets up." He realized his mistake the moment Ivy tensed, and he reached to move the cat. "I'm sorry," he said, then stilled when Ivy stopped him.

Her eyes were clear but glimmered as she held his gaze. "I know what you meant." She looked down when the cat's purr grew louder. Apple rolled to her back and stretched. "I don't want to leave either."

He laughed in relief but caught Ivy's hand before she dared to stroke the cat's exposed belly. "Don't fall for that one. It's definitely a trap."

THE END

ABOUT THE AUTHOR

Michelle Bolanger is a Christian author of contemporary and speculative fiction. She also writes non-fiction articles that share the hope of Christ through daily life lessons as a wife, author, and child of God. In addition to her writing, she is also a talented vocalist and enjoys painting. She lives in small town Ohio with her husband. Together, they enjoy going on long cruises, motorcycle rides along side roads and back roads, and cheering for their favorite professional hockey teams.

After 30+ years of mid-level management in banking and finance, Michelle left the corporate life to pursue her creative passions. She has co-lead Biblical courses on personal finance and budgeting, and served as the women's ministry co-ordinator for her local church where she crafted Bible studies and taught women how to apply Biblical principles to their daily lives. As a vocalist, she has served as a member of her church's worship team, leading the congregation into a deeper connection with God through song.

She began her publishing journey in 2015 with her urban fantasy debut novel, *"The Kiss"* the first book in a young adult series now titled *"The Divided Hearts Series."* She also published the first two stand alone contemporary novels in a collection of gritty, hot button stories that follow characters who come to faith in Christ after walking through some topics most Christian novelists won't write about. She tackles topics like LGBTQ, human trafficking, abortion, and adultery.

Michelle and her husband host a small group Bible study in their home once a week, and she has plans to expand her teaching and encouraging opportunities in the future by organizing an in person writer's group for writers of all levels in her local area. Her greatest desire is to demonstrate the hope of faith in Christ by sharing the lessons God is teaching her as she continues to publish new stories, grow her business, and encourage other writers and women in their giftings and callings.

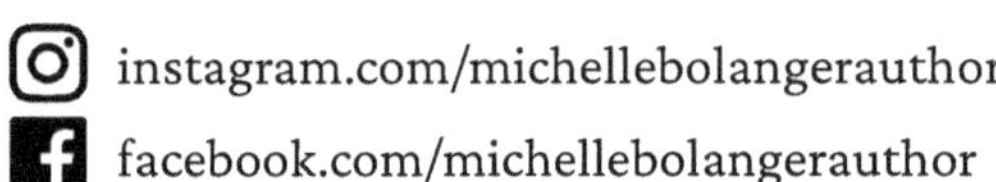

instagram.com/michellebolangerauthor
facebook.com/michellebolangerauthor

CONNECT WITH MICHELLE

Find me online:
Website: michellebolanger.com
Socials: @michellebolangerauthor
Email: Michelle@risenfiction.com